For Alicia – L.J.

For my ever-supportive parents – E.F.

In a small town on the banks of Lake Laloozee lives the world's greatest flamingo detective. His name is **Fabio**. He's not tall or strong, but slight and pink. And he's very, very clever.

At his side for every case is his friend and associate, **Gilbert**, a giraffe terrible at the art of disguise but good at asking questions – sometimes even the right ones.

Chapter 1

The bell rang as Fabio and Gilbert stepped into Alfonso's, the small and exclusive jeweller's shop. Alfonso's was as much part of the history of Laloozee as the Hotel Royale or Plume Street, where Fabio's detective agency was based.

'I'll be with you in one moment, gentlemen,' said Alfonso, who was an ageing tortoise with an unhurried way of speaking.

Fabio tipped his hat and he and Gilbert browsed the expensive jewellery as Alfonso dealt with his customer, a stylish desert fox.

'Good luck, my dear,' he said, carefully handing her a package. **'If your mother could see you now …'**

The fox smiled. 'Thank you, Mr Alfonso. It's a pleasure doing business with you.'

Fabio tipped his hat again as the fox sashayed out of the shop.

Alfonso turned his attention to Fabio and Gilbert. **'How may I be of service, gentlemen?'** he asked.

'It's my pocket watch, Alfonso,' said Gilbert, lolloping towards him. 'It seems to be on the blink.' He gave the watch a shake and then rested it on the counter.

Alfonso delicately picked it up and examined it through his eyeglass.

'I don't see these much any more,' he said. **'It's nothing too serious. I'll fix it now, if you don't mind waiting a minute.'**

'Not at all,' said Gilbert, trying his best not to be impatient. He felt sure,

at Alfonso's pace, it was going to take
more than a minute.

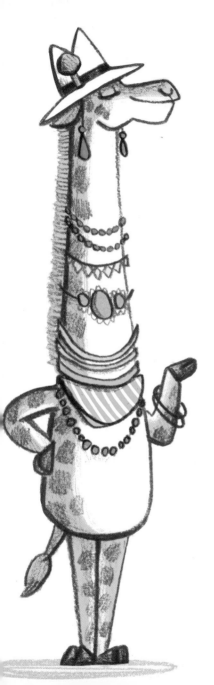

As Alfonso steadily made his way to his workshop, Fabio and Gilbert continued to look around. Gilbert tried a few things on.

'What do you think he meant when he said he doesn't see these much any more?' asked Gilbert. 'That's top of the range, that watch. Or at least it was.'

'And now its time is up,' murmured Fabio, who wasn't properly listening. Something through the shop window had caught his eye. Maybe it was a trick of the light, or maybe …

'What have you spotted now?' asked Gilbert. 'Don't you ever relax?'

'I may have spotted something, as you say,' replied Fabio. 'Or it may be nothing. A good brain, my dear friend, is always working, even when it knows it is going on holiday.'

Gilbert couldn't think of anything clever to say to that, but was saved

by Alfonso returning from his workshop.

'Your watch is ready, sir,' he said.

'I say,' said Gilbert, removing a pair of pearl earrings, 'you were very trusting leaving us in the shop alone. What if we'd tried to make off with all this valuable jewellery?'

'Well,' said Alfonso, **'you have an honest face.'**

Gilbert beamed and picked up his pocket watch.

'Cripes, is that the time? Fabio,

we'd better hurry or we'll miss our train. How much do I owe you?'

'**No charge,**' replied Alfonso. '**I just need some advice from the world's greatest flamingo detective.**'

'He's going to the Coral Coast with me and he's going to be late!' exclaimed Gilbert.

'But I would be delighted to assist when I return …'

Alfonso looked crestfallen. '**That might be too late.**'

'We're staying at the Coconut Palm Resort if you need me,' said Fabio.

Alfonso nodded slowly.

'Why did you tell him where we're staying?' asked Gilbert as he sped them through the back streets of Laloozee in his sports car.

'There was something bothering him,' Fabio replied.

'You're always overthinking things, Fabio. This is why you need a holiday!

By the way, what did you see on the other side of the street when we were at Alfonso's?' asked Gilbert, taking a corner at full speed.

Fabio clung to the car door for dear life. 'I thought I saw someone from the past,' he replied.

'How nice,' said Gilbert.

'Please can you drive more slowly, my friend?'

'Sorry!' Gilbert apologised, hitting the brakes.

'If it was who I thought it was, Gilbert,' Fabio continued, 'it was definitely not nice.'

There was no time for Gilbert to ask more, because they'd arrived at the Laloozee Central Train Station and they had a train to catch.

And not just any train – the Ostrich Express.

Chapter 2

The gleaming and magnificent Ostrich Express was by far the fastest locomotive in the world. A journey on the train promised the passenger an experience of true luxury and comfort.

The guard's whistle blew and steam filled the platform as Gilbert, directed by Fabio, loaded their baggage. Fabio helped him leap on board as the train began to chug its way majestically out of the station.

Fabio and Gilbert squeezed along the corridor past their fellow passengers until they found their compartment, number 13. Gilbert flopped down on the bottom bunk.

'You know what your trouble is, Gilbert?' mused Fabio as he carefully unpacked.

'No,' said Gilbert. 'What's my trouble?'

'You pack too much,' Fabio teased him.

'But I've only packed what I need,' Gilbert replied.

'A bucket and spade?' asked Fabio. 'Will your niece and nephew be joining us?'

'They're for me!' replied Gilbert, feeling slightly injured.

Fortunately for both of them there was a knock on the door.

'The dining car is now open,' the steward informed them, pretending he hadn't noticed Gilbert's bucket and spade. Gilbert kicked them under his bunk. He was regretting packing them.

'I could do with something to eat,'

said Fabio. 'How about you, Gilbert?'

'I'm starving!' Gilbert replied, the prospect of food making him suddenly feel much happier.

Fabio and Gilbert were not the first of the passengers to arrive in the opulent dining car. It was almost full.

The waiter showed them to their table and Fabio ordered two glasses of the finest pink lemonade.

Gilbert gazed out of the window. The sun was setting. Laloozee was already well behind them.

'Home is just a few twinkling lights in the distance now,' he said.

'Yes, and ahead of us,' said Fabio, 'the savannah turns to desert, and then finally we will reach the Coral Coast.'

'What if we get stuck in a sand dune?' asked Gilbert, sipping his lemonade.

'It is most unlikely,' said Fabio, 'but if

we do, I'm sure your bucket and spade will come in handy.'

Gilbert was about to respond when they were interrupted.

'May I sit here? The train is very full tonight and there's nowhere else for me to sit.'

Fabio recognised the speaker immediately. It was the desert fox from Alfonso's.

'Certainly,' said Fabio as both he and Gilbert stood up.

'My name is Zazie,' said the fox, taking a seat.

'This is Fabio, the world's greatest flamingo detective,' said Gilbert, pointing at his friend. Fabio nodded modestly. 'And I'm Gilbert.'

'The world's greatest ... ?' asked Zazie.

'I'm not the world's greatest anything, I'm afraid,' said Gilbert.

'But you are very good at asking questions,' said Fabio encouragingly.

Gilbert beamed.

Fabio ordered an extra glass of pink lemonade for their guest.

'May I say, what a beautiful pendant you're wearing,' Fabio complimented Zazie after they'd ordered their food.

Zazie nervously touched the pendant hanging from her neck.

'Yes, it's as big as an egg!' Gilbert marvelled.

'This is the Laloozee Ruby,' she said.
'I shouldn't really be wearing it. It's very
valuable, you see, but I thought, as we're
on a train, what could possibly happen
to it?'

'I heard there was a legend about the
Laloozee Ruby,' said Fabio.

'Yes, there is,' said Zazie. 'If you believe in that sort of thing. It says that the wearer must have a true heart. If they don't, the ruby will find itself a new home. It's all nonsense, of course, but people like stories so it should help me. I'm selling it, you see.'

'Oh, what a shame!' said Gilbert.

'The money from the sale will pay for a new wing at the Laloozee Infirmary. The auction is the day the train arrives at the Coral Coast,' Zazie smiled.

'Gosh,' said Gilbert. 'It must be worth a lot of money!' He was about to ask

Zazie if he'd seen her somewhere before, when the waiter arrived.

'Would you be interested in dessert?'

'Of course!' cheered Gilbert. 'Dessert in the desert, why not? Always room for pudding!'

Fabio jovially rolled his eyes at his friend as the waiter handed them the menus.

All of a sudden, the train braked sharply, throwing the waiter off balance and causing much upset with the rest of the diners in the carriage.

'Raspberry ripple!' were Gilbert's

last words as his head banged against the window and he was knocked unconscious.

In seconds, the train had shuddered to a complete stop.

Gilbert was out for the count. Fabio fanned him with the dessert menu and when that didn't work he threw a glass of pink lemonade over his friend.

'Black Forest gateau,' Gilbert mumbled as he came to.

'I'll look after Gilbert,' Zazie assured Fabio. 'You go and find out what's happened.'

Fabio tipped his hat and headed to the front of the train to see what had caused it to stop so suddenly. As he stepped on to the desert sand he was surprised by the coolness of the night. The sky was full of stars and the moon was a thin crescent.

He hurried towards a group of stewards. There was a great deal of

commotion. Only a few paces away from the buffers, gagged and tied to the tracks, was an elephant.

Chapter 3

'Untie him,' ordered Fabio, taking charge. Several members of the train's staff leaped into action and did their best to free the captive. The poor little elephant was frightened and made the ostrich's job even more difficult as he trumpeted loudly and resisted their attempts to free him.

Fabio approached the elephant softly and soothed his brow.

'My name is Fabio,' he introduced himself, undoing the gag in the elephant's mouth. 'What's your name?'

The young elephant blinked at Fabio.

'Shane,' he said at last.

'Shane, who did this to you?' Fabio asked as he removed the ties that held the young elephant to the rails.

'Bandits, sir, horrible bandits.' A big tear fell from his eye and his bottom lip trembled. 'I want my mummy!' he wailed.

Just then, out of the dark, ears flapping, came five elephants. The lead elephant trumpeted.

'Mummy!' Shane called out.

'Just one thing.' Fabio stopped him. 'What did the gang look like?'

'Nasty hyenas, and a … a horrible spotty …'

'Leopard?'

'Yeah, a horrible leopard.'

'Thank you, Shane. You can go now.'

Shane ran towards his mother. They looped their trunks together and embraced.

The mother elephant thanked Fabio, and Shane and his family disappeared into the night.

Fabio sighed with relief, but a chill breeze ruffled his feathers and his instincts told him that the night's dramas weren't over yet.

As if on cue, a terrible scream pierced the night sky.

'AAAAAAAAAAGH!'

It came from the dining car.

In the distance the eerie laugh of a hyena responded.

Fabio hurriedly climbed back on board the Ostrich Express. A quick glance out of the window made him catch his breath. The lights from the carriage shone on the trackside and picked out the unmistakeable silhouette of a leopard.

As he returned to the chaos of the dining car he didn't need to be told what he would find.

The Laloozee Ruby was gone.

Chapter 4

Zazie was clasping her neck where the ruby had once hung.

'What am I going to do? The infirmary is depending on me and now look what's happened! This is all my fault! I should never have worn the pendant. The thief just pulled it from my neck.'

'No, no!' protested Gilbert. 'It was my fault, I should have prevented this from happening. Oh, Fabio, I've let the side

down.' Gilbert hung his head in shame.

'You did no such thing,' said Fabio. 'This was the work of a criminal mastermind. Tell me exactly what happened.'

'I don't really know,' Gilbert lamented. 'I was still slightly dizzy from hitting my head.'

'It happened in an instant,' Zazie prompted him. 'I was targeted because I was so close to the carriage doors. I didn't hear anyone board the train. It must have been one of those cat burglars. Then there was a tug on my neck and I looked down and the ruby had disappeared.

That's when I screamed.'

Fabio turned to the rest of the diners. 'Has anyone else had anything stolen?'

Their fellow passengers all checked but no one else had any items missing.

Fabio narrowed his eyes. 'Gilbert, go and fetch your bucket while I speak to the train driver.'

'My bucket?' Gilbert scratched his head in confusion, then with alarm he realised something. 'I've got a huge bump!' He felt the other side of his head. 'Cripes, I've got two!' he exclaimed.

'Gilbert, you've always had those,' Fabio comforted him.

'Oh, right. Good. Yes, I remember now. Phew!'

Gilbert did as he was asked and made his way back to compartment 13 to fetch his bucket as Fabio headed in the opposite direction, to the front of the train.

The train driver was stoking the engine, in preparation for the Ostrich Express to move off. He didn't take kindly to the interruption, as he took great pride in keeping good time and the night's events risked delaying their journey. Still, he'd heard of Fabio and he listened carefully to what he said.

At the end of their discussion he nodded in agreement.

Fabio met Gilbert back in the dining car just as the train started moving again. There was a cheer from the passengers – no one enjoyed being a sitting duck when there were bandits about. They felt much safer now that they were back under way.

'Ladies and gentlemen, if I may have your attention.' Everyone dutifully quietened down and all eyes were on the flamingo detective.

'As you may know, there has been a terrible theft on board this train tonight. I believe the culprit is none other than Janice the Claw.'

There was a collective gasp from the passengers.

'As you know, Janice has been on the run since she broke out of the Laloozee jail. She must not be allowed to commit more crimes and so I propose to lay a trap to catch this thief, and I need your help,' continued Fabio.

This produced a murmur of excitement.

'Gilbert, pass me your bucket.'

Gilbert did as he was told. Fabio then removed his gold signet ring, the one with his family crest on it, and placed

it in the bucket.

'Gilbert, your watch, if you please,' said Fabio.

'Oh, er, all right,' said Gilbert, placing his pocket watch in the bucket. 'You will be careful with it, won't you? It was Uncle Herbert's.'

'I assure you no harm will come to your pocket watch,' said Fabio. He held the bucket

out to Zazie. 'Indeed, no harm will come to any of your possessions,' he added, looking at all the passengers. 'I just need to borrow them. You'll have them back tomorrow.'

Zazie removed her earrings and dropped them in. 'They're only cheap,' she apologised.

'They're perfect,' said Fabio. 'Thank you.'

Zazie then took the bucket from him and passed it round.

Reluctance gave way to curiosity and there soon followed the satisfying sound of jewellery and valuables being dropped into Gilbert's seaside bucket. By the time it was returned to Fabio it was brimming with shiny objects.

'Thank you, all,' said Fabio. 'May I bid you goodnight.'

As they walked through the carriage Gilbert overheard a zebra exclaim, 'Goodness, what an evening! They'll never believe me when I tell them about this at choir practice.'

'Do you know, I've just realised where

I've seen Zazie before,' said Gilbert. 'She was in Alfonso's!'

'Quite so,' said Fabio.

'Oh, you already knew that,' said Gilbert, closing the door to their compartment. 'I thought I was being quite clever then. So, what's the plan?'

'Well, my friend, you gave me the idea,' replied Fabio.

'I did?!' Gilbert felt a little better about that. 'Um, so how did I do that then?'

'Gilbert,' said Fabio. 'We're going to get stuck in a sand dune.'

'We are?' asked Gilbert. 'Cripes!'

'Soon after daybreak we will reach the Canyon of Oblivion,' Fabio informed him. 'We're going to pile up some rocks and sand and make it look like the train is stuck. You made me think of this, with your sand dune comment earlier.'

Gilbert felt quite proud.

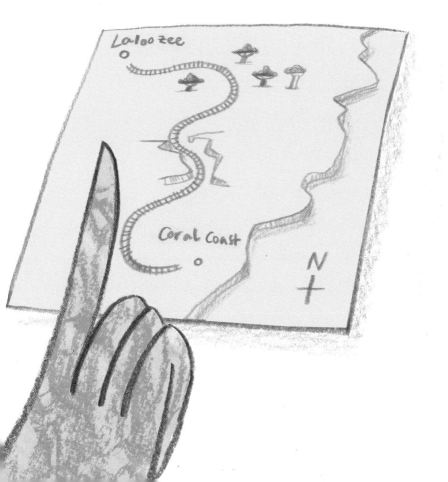

'We are then going to place the bucket of jewels on the other side of the sand dune,' Fabio explained. 'Janice and her gang may know it's a trap, but they will not be able to resist. They will be lured in by their love of all things shiny.'

'But won't they just run away when they have the treasure?' asked Gilbert.

'Ah, well that's where the second part of the plan comes in,' said Fabio.

'Oh, yes?' said Gilbert.

'I'll tell you all about that part in the morning,' said Fabio. 'Goodnight, my friend.'

'Goodnight,' said Gilbert.

Chapter 5

The Ostrich Express travelled swiftly through the night. As the sun rose over the desert the famous steam train approached the Canyon of Oblivion. Fabio and Gilbert were in the driver's cab to see it.

'This is mining country,' Fabio informed Gilbert. 'In fact,' he said, 'this is most likely where the Laloozee Ruby was first discovered.'

'Goodness,' said Gilbert. 'We should tell Zazie that.'

'I very much doubt she'd be interested,' replied Fabio.

The train entered the canyon and instantly it was much cooler. The Ostrich Express was now in deep shade and the canyon sides seemed to be getting closer.

In minutes, the walls of the canyon were within touching distance.

'Somewhere along this stretch?' asked the driver.

'Yes,' agreed Fabio. 'Put the brakes

on now,' he said as the canyon opened
out ahead.

When the train had come to a standstill,
the passengers were asked to remain on
board as the guards, stewards, waiters and
even the pastry chef jumped off the train.

Fabio had given them their instructions. They began to build the barricade.

'Make it look like a rockfall,' Fabio reminded them.

As they set to work, Fabio and Gilbert walked ahead a few paces. With the train and the barricade behind them Fabio set the bucket on the tracks.

'Fabio?'

'Yes, Gilbert?'

'Won't Janice and her gang just be able to pick up the bucket of jewels and run off the way they came, in the opposite direction of the train?'

'Yes,' said Fabio. 'That's what I'm hoping they will do.'

'Oh,' said Gilbert. 'But who is going to catch them?'

'We are!' replied Fabio. He gestured and a group of eager Ostrich Express employees came over.

'Follow me,' Fabio said.

'But where are we going?' asked Gilbert.

'To the old mine,' Fabio informed him.

A little further along the railway track there was a junction. Fabio led Gilbert and his team along the disused line, which led into a tunnel in the side of the canyon.

'What are we doing here?' asked Gilbert.

'We're looking for …' Fabio paused and looked around. 'Torch, please!'

The most junior steward produced a torch.

'This!' said Fabio triumphantly as the beam of the torch rested on a dusty old handcar.

'What does it do?' asked Gilbert.

'I'll show you,' said Fabio. 'Have you brought the tablecloths like I asked?'

'Yes!' said the assembled team.

'And have you tied them together, like I instructed you?'

'Yes!'

'Then climb on board,' said Fabio.

Everyone climbed on to the handcar.

'You power it by pushing these levers,' Fabio informed Gilbert as the pastry chef and the junior steward pushed the levers.

'See, it's like a seesaw,' he said.

'When was the last time you were on a seesaw?' asked Gilbert.

'You do ask too many questions,' joked Fabio as they began to pick up speed.

'We don't want to go too far,' he told them. 'About here should be fine.'

They stopped just before the railway track left the tunnel and joined the main line through the canyon. They were well hidden by a conveniently located rock.

'Now we wait,' whispered Fabio.

The sun began to beat down into the canyon and the cool of the morning started to wear off.

'How much longer do you think it'll be?' asked Gilbert.

'Now the sun is up, the jewels in your bucket will begin to glisten,' Fabio whispered in reply. 'Their lure will be too strong for Janice and her gang to resist.'

Sure enough, a lone hyena came into view, walking past the tunnel entrance where Fabio and his team were hiding. He sniffed the air.

Soon he was followed by two more scraggy-looking criminals. They made Gilbert's skin crawl. Then a further two

appeared. Finally, behind them slinked none other than Janice the Claw. Around her neck she wore the Laloozee Ruby.

Fabio signalled to wait.

The gang passed by and no one said a word. Then on Fabio's nod the team began to move.

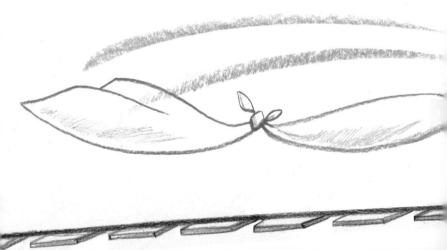

As Janice and the hyenas started to run towards the train, Fabio gestured that they should go faster. The junior steward and the pastry chef did their best. The Ostrich Express, barricade and bucket were now in view. The leading hyenas hunkered down and approached

the bucket suspiciously. The first one sniffed it and then let out a vicious laugh. Grabbing hold of the handle, he lifted it off the ground.

'Forward!' shouted Fabio, snatching Gilbert's cane and waving it in the air. The handcar accelerated as the steward and the pastry chef frantically pumped the handles.

'Ready!' commanded Fabio, banging the cane on the floor of the handcar. The ostriches threw the tablecloths out wide, as though the handcar had wings.

'Now!' ordered Fabio, and the tied-together tablecloths flew through the air and landed on the unsuspecting hyenas.

'Got them!' cheered Gilbert.

However, Janice, who had hung back, was able to free herself. She turned to look at her assailants.

'You!' she cried. 'You won't catch me, Fabio!' And she jumped on to the Ostrich Express, climbed on to its roof and sprinted towards the rear of the train.

Chapter 6

Fabio leaped on to the roof in pursuit.

'I'm coming too,' cried Gilbert, clambering down from the handcar.

Fabio was able to hop lightly from one carriage to the next, but it was an effort to keep up with the agile leopard.

Gilbert was having a terrible time. His fear of heights was kicking in and he was wobbling on his long legs.

'Whoa!'

Janice had reached the end of the train, but Fabio was catching up fast.

'You know you won't catch me again,' Janice sneered.

She turned to leap off the train to freedom just as Gilbert called out –

'Help, Fabio, I'm stuck!'

Gilbert had become wedged

between two carriages. Fabio knew he had to go to his friend's assistance.

Janice smirked but just before she leaped Fabio reached out Gilbert's cane, catching her necklace.

Janice looked on in horror as Fabio lifted the Laloozee Ruby clear from her neck. There was nothing she could do.

She was already falling. She landed heavily. Knowing she'd have to run or be caught, she ran.

Fabio rushed over to Gilbert.

'I'm so sorry, Fabio,' said Gilbert. 'If I hadn't got stuck, you'd have caught Janice the Claw.'

'There's time enough for that now we've got the ruby back,' said Fabio.

It took three stewards to help Gilbert become unstuck.

'Let's get you comfortable,' suggested Fabio, once Gilbert had been freed. He led him through to the dining car and ordered two glasses of pink lemonade.

They were met by a cheer from the passengers. Fabio gave a small bow in thanks.

The guard approached. 'We've secured the prisoners in the baggage compartment.'

'There's a baggage compartment?' asked Gilbert, sipping his lemonade.

'And here's the bucket of jewellery.' The guard handed it over to Fabio.

'Ooh, good, Uncle Herbert's watch, I felt lost without it,' said Gilbert, picking out his family heirloom.

He then set about returning everyone else's valuables and had nearly finished when Zazie appeared.

'Here are your earrings,' said Gilbert.

'And my necklace?' she asked, ignoring Gilbert and looking straight at Fabio.

Fabio handed her the Laloozee Ruby.

'You take good care of that,' said Fabio. 'It knows what's in your heart.'

Zazie walked off without so much as thanking him.

'She seemed so charming before,' commented Gilbert.

'Mmm,' agreed Fabio.

Chapter 7

'Well, that was an eventful journey,' marvelled Gilbert as they climbed into their taxi at the Coral Coast.

'To the Coconut Palm Resort,' Fabio ordered the driver.

'The police were pleased we'd caught those hyenas, weren't they?' said Gilbert.

'Yes, but Janice the Claw is still at large,' Fabio reminded him.

'Yes, quite,' agreed Gilbert, still feeling guilty about that.

The Coconut Palm Resort was all Gilbert had hoped it would be. Fabio checked in for them while Gilbert dipped his toe in the pool.

'We have a message for you, sir,' said the clerk, handing Fabio a note. Fabio read it and got straight on the telephone.

When he'd finished making his calls he found Gilbert.

'Gilbert! We have to hurry!'

'Why?' asked Gilbert, who'd already bagged the best sunlounger.

'I've had a message from Alfonso …'

'What did that slowcoach want?'

'The Laloozee Ruby belongs to him!'

'Really?!'

'Yes, and he's worried someone's going to steal it!'

'Again?!'

Fabio was already hailing a taxi.

'Listen, I haven't got time to explain. We have to get down to the auction, it's about to start,' said Fabio urgently.

'Shouldn't we go in disguise?' asked

Gilbert. 'Perhaps a change of hat?'

'Look, here's a taxi – climb in, Gilbert, we have to hurry.'

Gilbert had to leave his inflatable on the steps of the hotel.

'Why is this taxi going so slowly?' complained Fabio.

'Now you want someone to drive fast!' Gilbert harrumphed.

'Stop here!' Fabio ordered the driver. He quickly paid and they both jumped out and ran the rest of the way to the auction rooms.

They hurried into the packed showroom and took the last two seats at the back. Fabio could see Zazie sitting centre front.

They were just in time.

'Lot number twenty-six,' the

auctioneer informed the room. 'The famous Laloozee Ruby.'

His assistant lifted the ruby necklace, which was displayed on a velvet cushion, so everyone could see.

'Rumour has it,' continued the auctioneer, 'that the wearer of this ruby must have a true heart, or it will find itself a more suitable owner. So buyer beware!' he joked. 'Who'll start the bidding, at one hundred guineas?'

A gazelle in the third row raised her paddle.

'One hundred and fifty?'

A buffalo at the back winked.

Then there was a telephone bid and the bidding rapidly increased.

A rattlesnake by the window tipped his hat.

'Four hundred guineas, anyone?' asked the auctioneer.

The room fell silent. Fabio held his breath for the next bid as a shadow passed over the auction room. Above them was Janice the Claw. With a flick of her wrist she let down a rope and abseiled through the skylight.

The auctioneer's assistant fainted from the shock.

Janice reached for the velvet cushion and clasped the Laloozee Ruby in her paw.

There were shrieks and wails from the audience. Gilbert rushed towards the front of the auction room, but in his enthusiasm, he tripped over his own feet. Like a felled tree, he came crashing to the ground and headbutted Janice, knocking her out.

The Laloozee Ruby tumbled from her grasp and the auctioneer lunged to retrieve it.

In the commotion, it was only Fabio who noticed Zazie going against the crowd and leaving the auction house.

'Where do you think you're going?' he asked.

'Oh, get out of my way, you pesky pink detective.'

She pushed quickly past Fabio, but he was quicker, and he tripped her up with an outstretched foot.

She tried to scramble to her feet but she was too late. The police had arrived.

'Arrest the leopard,' Fabio told them. 'And this fox.'

Chapter 8

'We're on holiday, but I can't go swimming!' moaned Gilbert, whose foot was in plaster.

'Well, if you will go rushing about the place,' said Fabio with a smile. 'You can't help catch master criminals and always avoid danger, you know.'

'I did help, didn't I?' asked Gilbert.

'You were magnificent, my friend.'

'Explain to me again how you knew

Zazie was behind it all,' asked Gilbert.

'Well,' said Fabio. 'I first suspected her when she said the pendant was pulled from her neck but when I recovered it from Janice the chain wasn't broken. She had in fact given the necklace to Janice, her accomplice.

'I also thought it was strange that no one else had any valuables stolen. How had Janice known the Laloozee Ruby would be on our train that night unless someone had told her? Zazie had asked to sit at our table because ours was closest to the door. It was, of course, unfortunate for her that the table she needed was occupied by the world's greatest flamingo detective, no?'

'So Zazie had the ruby because Alfonso had asked her to sell it for him at the auction … ?'

'Yes, because he couldn't leave his shop, and he's getting on a bit. Zazie's mother had been one of his best customers. She'd helped him build up his business and he'd promised her he'd always keep an eye on Zazie. Zazie, of course, jumped at the chance to sell the ruby for him. She has expensive taste and her mother had left all her wealth to the infirmary, so she needed the cash but she didn't want anyone to accuse her of stealing it. That's when she got word to Janice and they hatched their plot together.'

'So it was Janice you thought you'd spotted on the other side of the street?'

'Precisely,' said Fabio. 'I had her locked up once before but she escaped. This time, they assure me, she'll do her time.'

'It's very generous of Alfonso to donate the ruby like that,' mused Gilbert.

'Yes. He told me that his grandson, Alfie, was very ill when he was born and the infirmary saved his life. Alfonso said it was the least he could do. In fact, he'd been inspired by Zazie's mother to make the donation, but he began not to trust Zazie. She wanted to sell the ruby in a hurry and kept pestering him about it. He'd thought of asking me to tail her, but unfortunately he was too late.'

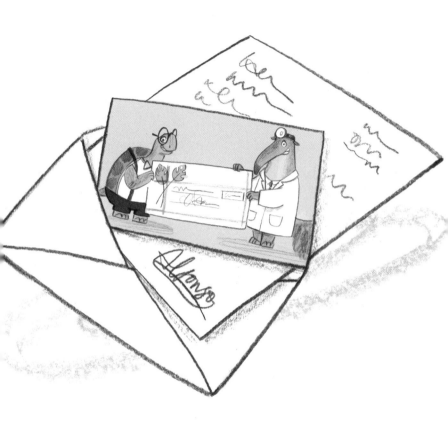

'Did Alfonso manage to sell the ruby in the end?' asked Gilbert, taking a sip of his pink lemonade.

'Yes, I just found out that it sold for a

thousand guineas, well above the price he was hoping for.'

Gilbert whistled in amazement.

'They'll be able to do a lot with that at the infirmary,' smiled Fabio. 'Apparently, a wealthy hippopotamus bought the ruby for his daughter.'

'That's nice!' said Gilbert. 'And how is the world's greatest flamingo detective enjoying his holiday?' he asked.

'It's just what I needed,' replied Fabio, raising his glass to his friend.

HE'S SLIGHT, HE'S PINK AND HE'S VERY, VERY CLEVER ...

Turn over for a sneak peek at Fabio's first case!

AVAILABLE NOW

Chapter 1

As the sun began to set, Fabio and his great friend Gilbert walked through the splendid doors of the Hotel Royale. It was time for a cool glass of pink lemonade. Little did they know, as they were greeted by Smith, the hotel's owner, that this pleasant place was about to be hit by a big mystery.

'Good evening, gentlemen.'

Smith led them through the grand

but entirely empty lobby to the terrace at the back of the hotel, where they took their usual table by the pool.

At the bar a rhino rustled her newspaper.

Smith was a grumpy old vulture. Fabio had known him for many years. He ran the hotel with his sister, Penelope, who was a temperamental chef. Penelope's daughter Violet had just started working at the hotel too.

'It's very quiet in here this evening,' commented Fabio, taking note of his surroundings.

'Yes,' agreed Smith unhappily. 'Business is slow. Violet has decided to hold a talent contest to liven the place up a bit.' He presented Fabio and Gilbert with the lemonade menu and gave a small bow. 'It won't work,' he added gloomily. Smith, Fabio knew, did not welcome Violet's schemes. She was going to have a tough time changing things at the hotel.

Fabio spotted Violet putting up a poster advertising the contest.

Smith beckoned her over. 'Violet, come and say hello to Mr Fabio and his good friend Gordon.'

'Gilbert,' Gilbert corrected him. He'd been correcting Smith for years.

'Hello, Mr Fabio, Mr Gilbert,' said Violet. 'Lovely evening, isn't it?'

The rhino at the bar thrust her nose over the top of her newspaper. 'I knew it!' she exclaimed. 'You're that pink detective, aren't you?'

Fabio politely tipped his hat. 'Fabio, the world's greatest flamingo detective at your service, madam.'

'The name's Daphne. But everyone calls me the General. I'm just back from safari. Shall I join you?'

Without waiting for a response, the General put her newspaper under her arm, bustled over to their table and took a seat between Fabio and Gilbert. It was a bit of a squash.

No sooner had the General sat down, than there was an enormous splash as a hippo launched herself off the diving board and into the pool, drenching everyone at the table.

THE ADVENTURES OF PUG!

AVAILABLE NOW